PROJECT
BOLLYWOOD

PROJECT BOLLYWOOD

MAHTAB NARSIMHAN

ORCA BOOK PUBLISHERS

Published in Canada and the United States in 2022 by Orca Book Publishers.
orcabook.com

Library and Archives Canada Cataloguing in Publication
Title: Project Bollywood / Mahtab Narsimhan.
Names: Narsimhan, Mahtab, author.
Series: Orca currents.
Description: Series statement: Orca currents
Identifiers: Canadiana (print) 20210182776 | Canadiana (ebook) 20210182814 |
ISBN 9781459832114 (softcover) | ISBN 9781459832121 (PDF) |
ISBN 9781459832138 (EPUB)
Classification: LCC PS8627.A77 P76 2022 | DDC jC813/.6—dc23

Library of Congress Control Number: 2021934060

Summary: In this high-interest accessible novel for middle-grade readers,
a young filmmaker tries to recreate a Bollywood film for a school project.

Orca Book Publishers is committed to reducing the consumption of
nonrenewable resources in the production of our books. We make
every effort to use materials that support a sustainable future.

Orca Book Publishers gratefully acknowledges the support for its publishing
programs provided by the following agencies: the Government of Canada,
the Canada Council for the Arts and the Province of British Columbia
through the BC Arts Council and the Book Publishing Tax Credit.

Edited by Tanya Trafford
Design by Ella Collier
Cover artwork by Getty Images/Mayur Kakade
and Getty Images/Jonathan Knowles
Author photo by Dean MacDonnell of MacDonnell Photography

Printed and bound in Canada.

25 24 23 22 • 1 2 3 4

For Tanya. Who gets my stories.

Chapter One

Salman curled his scrawny biceps in time to the thumping beat of the dance music. He checked himself out in the gym mirror and generally liked what he saw. A handsome, if *slightly*—okay, *very* thin—young man. He had work to do though. He had the same name as a famous Bollywood star. He wanted to be as famous as that Salman Khan. He added squats while continuing to work his arms.

"Salman, your mother is on the phone," said Ramesh, walking into his room. He held out the cordless phone. "She said she tried calling your cell phone, but no one picked up."

Salman grabbed a towel and wiped the sweat off his face. Ramesh, who basically ran the Khan household, turned down the volume on the stereo.

"You could have knocked before coming in," Salman snapped.

"I did, but how could you have heard me?" said Ramesh. His tone was soft.

Salman immediately felt bad for *his* tone of voice. It wasn't Ramesh's fault that he was trying hard to look like his hero, Salman the Star. And the music *had* been loud.

"Hi, Mom," he said. "Sorry, I was working out and didn't hear my phone. What time are you and Dad getting home?"

Ramesh started to tidy up Salman's room. Salman let him, moving toward the window.

"*What*? Mom, you promised you'd be home by the weekend. The blockbuster *Hungama* just opened. We were planning to see it all together. Remember?"

Salman noticed Ramesh standing in the doorway. He looked sad. Salman turned away from him, not wanting his pity. He wanted his parents to come home, but apparently that wasn't happening anytime soon. He placed the handset down and put it on *speaker*. He picked up his weights and started doing more curls.

"These buyers are very demanding," said his mom. "Your father and I are still negotiating the contract with the lawyers. We'll be working the whole weekend. I'm sorry, Salman. But why don't you invite your friends over? You said they loved watching Hindi movies with you."

"It's not the same as watching it with my family," said Salman coldly. "Your business always comes first."

"What do you want me to do? Shut down everything and just fly home?" his mom asked, her tone sharp. "You know what that would mean?" Salman rolled his eyes, even though his mom couldn't see him. He knew what came next. He'd heard it a million times before. "No more expensive gadgets for you. No video cameras, or editing software, or big monitors to screen your movies on. We'll stay home, live a modest life, and watch movies. Would you prefer that, Salman?"

Salman almost snorted. His parents had several companies that manufactured IT security equipment. These products and services were always in demand. Even if they retired now, they could all live comfortably for the rest of their lives. It didn't take a genius to figure that out. The fact was, his parents loved the luxuries money could buy, but above all they loved to work. *Thrived* on it. It was as important as the air they breathed. Their son, Salman figured, was more like a french fry to them. Fun to eat, but best had in small amounts.

"Okay, Mom, I get it," said Salman as he started doing some more squats. His mom was still talking, asking the usual questions about school, but he was in no mood to share. She was probably getting a more detailed report from Ramesh anyway.

"Salman? Are you there?"

"Yeah, Mom," he said. "But I have to go."

"Okay, love you, sweetheart," she replied.

"Bye, Mom," said Salman and disconnected the phone.

He picked up his cellphone. Three missed calls from Mom. None from Dad. Ramesh was the one looking out for him and he'd been rude to him for no reason. He felt bad for a second. He'd make it up to Ramesh later. He texted his best friend, Jason.

Want to hang out tonight?

Jason texted back almost immediately.

Can't. Have to babysit sibs. Check with Maya and Arman.

Maya and Arman were the other two of their group. If it weren't for them he'd be as invisible in school as he was at home. He fired them each a text. Neither responded.

Maya had so many extra-curricular activities going on, it was a wonder she had time to do homework. Arman was into biking and was making the most of fall. He wanted to get in as much time as he could before the snow made it tough to ride. He was probably out riding now. Sighing, Salman looked at the clock on his phone. He had time for a shower before lunch.

Lunch was delicious. Ramesh, born and brought up in Chennai, had mastered the art of the crispy dosa with spiced potato filling. Even his friends raved about Ramesh's cooking.

"Great food, as always, Ramesh. Sorry I snapped at you earlier," said Salman when he finished.

Ramesh nodded. "I understand. It mustn't be easy for you. But your parents have a lot of responsibilities on their shoulders. They have to make sure their employees are also looked after."

Salman felt the familiar irritation rising, and he fought to keep it down. "You don't need to make excuses for them," he said. "I'm fine and thanks to their hard work, I have everything I could need or want."

Ramesh didn't respond. He started clearing the table.

Salman got up and wandered into the media room. It had a giant-screen TV, a perfectly calibrated surround-sound system and soft lighting. It was impressive, but it was just one room in their fourteen-room mansion. They also had an indoor pool, a sauna, and gym. The manicured lawns behind the house were so huge it was hard to believe this place was right in the middle of a big North American city.

If this were a Hindi movie, their house would have belonged to a villain who had earned all his wealth through terrible and illegal means. But Salman's parents weren't villains. They were just missing. All the time.

Salman flopped onto the cream sofa in front of the TV. Instead of turning it on, he stared at the ceiling.

This house had *everything* a person could want.

Except people to share it with.

Chapter Two

Salman Khan, the popular Bollywood actor not the scrawny teenager, was fighting a bunch of villains in *Dabangg 3*. His punch went right through a steel door and landed on a gangster's face. In another scene, he kicked a bad guy, and the man flipped in the air three times before landing with a thud. Salman flexed his muscles and stood there while the gangster pleaded for mercy. The camera angled in for a close shot of the star as dramatic music played in the background.

Jason rolled on the floor of the media room, clutching his stomach and roaring with laughter. Arman crunched nonstop on potato chips. His eyes were glued to the action on the screen. Maya giggled into a pillow.

Salman smiled. Even though his friends thought Bollywood movie plots were corny and made no sense, they watched *all* the new ones with him. He loved them for it. He also made it a point to watch the movies again with Ramesh. The second viewing was so he could observe all the tiny details. One day he would produce, direct *and* star in his own productions. He would return to Mumbai, the birthplace of the world-famous Bollywood film industry. India produced the largest number of feature films in the world per year. One day, Salman would join the ranks of those producers.

Ramesh slipped into the room to replenish the snacks. Salman met his eyes and nodded his thanks.

Ramesh winked and nodded back. Then he slipped out again, no doubt busy with more chores.

Salman had no idea how Ramesh had tracked his friends down, but he had. Not only that, he'd rented the latest Salman Khan movie and prepared a table full of sweet and savory snacks. So now, instead of moping in his room on a Saturday night, Salman was enjoying the third installment in one of his favorite movie series with his friends.

The movie ended and the credits rolled. Salman muted the sound. "I really want to make a movie," he said.

"Don't they cost millions of bucks to produce?" asked Maya.

"You are talking to a guy who is rolling in cash," said Arman. "If anyone can afford to make a blockbuster, it is Salman. Right, brother?"

"Bro," said Jason. "If you're going to use the lingo, use it correctly, *bro*."

Arman rolled his eyes.

"Back to my movie," said Salman. "It doesn't have to be a major production. Just a small one. If I wrote out a script, would you all be in it? We could shoot it over the Christmas holidays. You don't want to be eating turkey and playing games all week. Right?"

Salman was sure he would be spending a lot of the Christmas holidays on his own. Mom and Dad would be working. But if he had a project to occupy himself, time would go by faster. It was the perfect time to make his movie. And who better to shoot it with than his buddies?

Maya jumped to her feet, flipped her curly hair with one hand and batted her eyelids. "The lead role is mine," she said. "I can totally dance around a tree in the rain."

"And I am your hero!" said Arman, punching the air in a mock fight.

"Hold it right there," said Salman, throwing a pillow at Arman. "If anyone's going to be the hero in my movie, it's me. You can be the villain."

"What about me?" asked Jason, stuffing a jalapeño popper into his mouth.

"You'll be my loyal buddy," said Salman. "We'll have a fun time together, but you're going to have to die somewhere in the middle so I can avenge your death." His brain was already churning with the possibilities of the script he had yet to write. Jason made a face.

Maya's phone chimed. She looked at the screen. "Have to go home. Mom's orders."

"Yeah, we have to go too," said Jason. "Awesome evening, Sal!"

"That was fun, bro," said Arman, grabbing another handful of chips. "But I don't think I want to be the villain. I want a better role."

Salman smiled. "You're welcome. And hey, I haven't even written the script yet. But I assure you, everyone will have a good role." As his friends filed out of the media room, he added, "I'll ask Ramesh to give you all a ride home."

"Thanks!" said Maya. "I didn't want to stand at the bus stop in the cold. The wind is really picking up."

"Wind does not bother a hero," said Arman, laughing, as he put on his jacket. He flexed both arms in the same pose as Salman Khan. The actor.

"You're still not getting the lead role, bro. Or the role of the loyal buddy," said Jason. "Right, Salman?"

Salman had returned with Ramesh. He was loving all this banter. He really wished his friends didn't have to leave. In a few minutes the house would be silent again. Quiet enough to hear his own heartbeat.

"I'll get the car," said Ramesh, walking out ahead of them.

"Hey, Sal, how are your parents?" asked Maya.

The question made Salman feel like someone had reached in and squeezed his heart. "They're fine. Still in China, negotiating some deal or other."

"They're not home a lot, are they?" said Jason. "You must really miss them."

A sharp nudge from Arman almost threw him off-balance.

Salman forced a smile. "I do, but I'm used to it by now. Ramesh is good company and I have *you* campers. Thank god Mr. Fodi grouped us together for that project last year. I could never have got through seventh grade without you all."

Maya slung an arm around Sal's shoulder and squeezed. The boys fist-bumped him.

"We got your back, bro," said Jason. "Maybe *I* can be the hero in your next film!"

Salman laughed and clapped Jason on the back. A horn honked outside. Ramesh was waiting. Salman opened the door and the sharp wind slid inside, chilling him to the bone. It was the beginning of November and already there was a hint of snow in the air. Maya, Jason and Arman ran to the car and scrambled inside. They all waved at Salman as Ramesh drove off down the long driveway. Despite the cold, Salman stood and watched the red taillights till they rounded a bend and disappeared. Then he shut the door. The house was so quiet.

He tidied up the media room and put away all the food, waiting for Ramesh to return. In his head were the beginnings of a great movie idea.

It would be the blockbuster of the century. He was sure of that.

Chapter Three

Ms. Lopez, who taught media arts, was Salman's favorite teacher. She allowed them to experiment with their assignments. And she gave marks for creativity. *Let your imaginations soar* was a frequently repeated instruction in her class. She was colorful in her teaching style and in her appearance. Today she was wearing baggy linen pants and a bright red tunic. Sparkly earrings peeped out from her mop of shoulder-length silver hair.

"Good morning, everyone," she said. "Settle down, please. I have a special project that I think you will enjoy." Her eyes twinkled.

Almost everyone in the class shut up. Ms. Lopez looked around the room. "You will have two weeks to create a group project to present to the class. It can be in any medium you like, but it should be built around some or all of the topics we've covered so far. I'm passing around a list of ideas to help you get started. If anyone has questions, come see me after class."

Salman felt like leaping onto the desk to dance to a Bollywood song playing in his head. He knew *exactly* what he wanted to do for his project.

"Salman!"

Salman snapped out of his daydream. The entire class was staring at him. "Yes, Ms. Lopez?"

"I called your name because you seemed very far away."

Salman felt his face grow hot. "Er, I'm sorry, Ms. Lopez. What did I miss?" Several people laughed.

Ms. Lopez shook her head, but her eyes were smiling. "You've been grouped together based on your last names."

Salman grinned at the good news. "Awesome! I've already started thinking about the project! I'm super excited."

"Now that's what I like to hear," she said. "I can't wait to see what your group comes up with."

Salman glanced around at his friends, who returned his smile. Once again, things were going his way. His friends, Arman Kazmi, Jason Lewis and Maya Maloney, would be in his group again because of their last names. They'd worked so well as a team when they'd first been grouped in Mr. Fodi's class the year before. They'd enjoyed each other's company and had become inseparable. Salman tried not to think about the year after this, when they'd move on to high school and be apart.

"So it's me, Maya, Jason and Arman," said Salman. "Right?"

"And Natalie," said Ms. Lopez.

Natalie Ming. Salman knew that name and it stood for trouble. Why couldn't her last name have started with *A* or *Z*? "Oh," he said weakly, glancing over at Natalie.

She gave him a nasty look in return.

At lunchtime, Salman sat in the cafeteria with his friends. "Cheer up," said Maya, dipping a sweet pepper into a small container of hummus. "Natalie's not so bad once you get to know her."

"Well, she doesn't have a problem with making her opinions known," said Jason through a mouthful of burger. "If she's got something to say, there's no stopping her."

"What do you mean?" asked Salman. He took a large bite of pizza. It was cheesy and gooey, just the way he liked it.

Jason tried to reply but his mouth was still full. He started to choke. Arman thumped him on the back. Jason waved him off. He took a sip of his drink and continued.

"The other day Natalie was practicing on the basketball court. Sergio tripped her accidentally but didn't say anything, just kept playing. She created such a stink that Coach Martin came racing out of his office. He made Sergio apologize and then banned him from the court for the day."

"She sounds like a pain in the butt," said Salman. He shoved the last bite of pizza into his mouth.

"Why, because she stood up for herself?" said Maya. "That's not fair. Sometimes I wish *I* was as strong as she is."

Salman shrugged. "Okay, let's talk about the project. I've got a great idea. I know you guys are super busy, so I volunteer to do most of the work. But I think you guys are going to *love* it. And if we all agree to it now, Natalie will have to get on board."

"Natalie does not *have* to do *anything*," said an icy voice. "Especially if she doesn't like it."

They all looked up. Natalie stood there, lunch tray in hand, glaring at them.

Chapter Four

"Hey, Nat," said Jason, wiping his greasy mouth with a napkin. "How's it going?"

"The name is Natalie," she said sternly. She then sat down at their table. She didn't wait to be invited. "So tell me, Salman. What are we doing for our project?"

Silence. Everyone looked at Salman. He'd barely told his friends about the project. He needed their buy-in before telling Natalie. But what if they hated the idea? There was no way Natalie would agree to it if they all disagreed. He wanted this so badly, his heart raced and his mouth was dry. Sweat trickled down his armpits.

"Go on," said Natalie, biting into a tuna sandwich. She looked at each member of the group.

Salman cleared his throat and gave it his best shot. "I was thinking of making a movie, Bollywood style. I have all the equipment for pre- and post-production. We could shoot it at my place."

"I *knew* you'd say that!" said Jason and Arman together.

Maya laughed. "So that was why you were in a fog when Ms. Lopez announced the assignment, yeah?"

Salman felt his face grow warm again. They knew him so well. But then, they were his best friends.

"What's 'Bollywood style'?" asked Natalie, tucking her straight black hair behind one ear. "I know you're talking about movies from India, but I've never seen one. So tell me what you mean."

Salman cleared his throat. Where to start? How could he describe everything he loved about a Hindi movie? The fun, the color, the comedy, the tragedy, the joy? The name "Bollywood" was a play on the name Hollywood. The *B* was for Bombay, now Mumbai, the largest city in India. That's where most of the movies were made. The producers believed in giving the audience their money's worth and packed every movie with as much emotion as they could. It was the best thing ever!

He opened his mouth and shut it again. Maya jumped in. "You'll have to trust the expert," she said, slipping her lunch box into her backpack. "And you have to *see* it to *get* it. No words could properly describe a Bollywood movie, right, Sal?

I still can't get over the last one we saw—*Da Bang*, yeah?"

"*Dabangg*," said Salman. "It means 'strong.' And thanks, that's exactly it. No words could do it justice."

"The man punched through a steel door!" said Jason, laughing. "I'd say he was strong."

Natalie looked around at each of them. "I don't know about this. It sounds a bit over the top."

Lunch break was almost over. Around them the noise levels rose as students started to head back to class. The smell of food was strong and slightly unpleasant.

"Why don't you all come over to my place tomorrow night," said Salman. "That will give me time to work on the script outline. And we can watch a movie together so Nat—sorry, *Natalie*"—Salman caught her eye—"has a better idea of what it is we're trying to do."

"Shouldn't everyone in the group get a chance to propose a project?" asked Natalie. "China has great operas. We could do one in ballet form. What if each of us proposed a project and took a vote?"

"I do *not* do ballet," said Arman. "No. Way."

"Ballet dancers have to be incredibly strong," said Natalie. "Don't shoot it down until you've tried it. It's not only fun but also a great workout." She raised an eyebrow and looked around the group again.

This was going nowhere, Salman thought. The bell rang, thankfully, and they all stood up. "Why don't you hear me out tomorrow?" said Salman. "Then, if most of us agree, we make a movie. If not, someone else can propose an idea. In fact, you should each come with your idea."

Salman knew it sounded like he was being open to other options. But he also knew that Jason had to babysit his younger brother and sister. Maya had a ton of activities going on—jazz, piano and singing lessons. Arman, who loved to bike, went out riding whenever he had free time. None of them had the kind of spare time that Salman had. He knew they would probably be happy to let someone else do most of the work. Not that they were lazy. They just did not have the same motivation. Natalie was the only one likely to oppose. He would need a brilliant script and three yeses.

The rest of the day was a blur as Salman outlined his script, cast the characters, and shot the movie. All in his head.

"My friends are coming over tomorrow," said Salman when Ramesh picked him up after school. He was seated in the back of their Mercedes while Ramesh expertly navigated the rush-hour traffic.

"On a school night?" said Ramesh. "Don't you have homework? Your mother will not like it."

"It's for a school project," said Salman. "I've decided to make a movie with the group, and we'll be shooting it at the house." His stomach clenched with excitement. His *own production*, for the very first time. The entire class would see it. It would be so fantastic, Ms. Lopez would insist they air it for the entire school. Once he uploaded it online, a producer in Bollywood might see it and beg him to join his studio as soon as he was done school. His career as a director slash producer was about to take off.

"Have you written a script?" asked Ramesh.

Salman tapped his temple. "It's all up here. It'll take me no time to write it out."

"Did you discuss it with your friends?" Ramesh glanced at Salman in the rearview mirror.

Salman met his eyes. "They haven't heard the pitch yet," he said. "But once they do, they'll love it. So can you make enough dinner for five? It'll be me, Jason, Arman, Maya, plus one more. This girl Natalie is also in our group."

"Why don't you write it together?" Ramesh suggested. "Get everyone's input."

"They don't have a clue how to write a Bollywood script," said Salman. "I've watched millions of movies. *I'm* the expert. Enough, Ramesh," he added, waving his hand. "I need to think."

They rode the rest of the way home in silence. Salman felt bad about shutting up Ramesh. He'd only been trying to help. But Salman did not want anyone's input in this project. *He* was the expert, not them. First Natalie and now Ramesh. Here he was, on the brink of launching his brilliant career, and all he got was negativity.

Sheesh!

Chapter Five

Salman worked hard on the script after dinner. He lost track of the time and when he went to grab himself a chicken-tikka roll, Ramesh appeared in the kitchen. He informed him that it was three in the morning. But it was daytime in China. Would he like to call his parents and explain to them why he was up so late on a school night?

"An artist does not keep track of the time!" Salman exclaimed.

Ramesh began to punch in numbers on his cellphone.

"All right, *all right*!" said Salman. "Can I at least finish my snack? I'm starving."

Ramesh's expression softened. "Want me to warm it up for you?"

"No thanks," said Salman and finished it in a few quick bites. "Good night."

"Good morning," said Ramesh.

They'd headed back to their rooms in silence.

Salman tried not to yawn as he looked at his friends gathered in the media room. Ramesh had provided a fabulous Indian meal to set the tone for the evening. Despite all Ramesh's nagging, Salman knew he was lucky to have someone like him in his life.

The gang had assumed their usual places. Arman was sprawled on the carpet in the middle of the room. Maya was hugging a pillow on the sofa by the window, her feet tucked under her. Jason sat on the floor, leaning back against the loveseat, within easy reach of the snacks. Salman always sat in the middle of the sofa centered in front of the screen. The sofa was also set just the right distance from the surround-sound system. It was the best spot to watch and listen to a movie.

Natalie sat alone in a chair, hands in her lap.

"Everyone ready to listen to my pitch for *Dostana*?" said Salman, passing around several sheets of paper. "That's the title. I've mapped out the basics—the storyline and the cast and whatnot."

"Go for it!" said Jason. The others nodded.

"What does 'dos-tana' mean?" asked Natalie.

"It's the Hindi word for friendship," said Salman. "But if you don't mind, I'd like to keep going without interruption. I can take questions at the end. Everyone have a copy?"

Everyone said yes except Natalie. She nodded but did not look happy.

"Ramesh!" Salman called out. "Please join us—you have a part in this too."

Ramesh hurried in from the kitchen and leaned against the wall near the door. Maya passed him a sheet. Everyone turned their attention to Salman.

"Okay, the movie opens on two friends. They are also struggling photographers, played by Jason and yours truly. They need to rent an affordable room in the city. They find one that they like, sublet by a girl played by Maya. But her wealthy father, played by Ramesh, will not allow it."

"Why not?" asked Maya. "It would be so cool to have two guys as roomies."

"In India, an unmarried girl cannot share an apartment with boys," said Salman. "It's definitely not cool."

"But this is a modern story, isn't it? A chance for us to show how things are more liberal now," said Natalie. "Or how things should be, at least."

"Can you all let me finish?" said Salman through gritted teeth.

Natalie sniffed loudly. Maya shrugged.

"The guys pretend they're gay to convince Maya's father that she's safe because they have no interest in his daughter," said Salman. "They play-act their deep love for each other."

Salman looked around the group. No one said a word. His eyes shifted to Ramesh, who also said nothing.

"Ramesh agrees to let the guys rent the room from his daughter," Salman continued. "Unfortunately, both guys fall in love with Maya. Each tries to woo her while the other sabotages his friend's chances with her. Maya thinks the boys are just being friendly and doesn't take them seriously. She meets Arman through her best friend Natalie—a poor girl jealous of her ultra-rich friend but hiding it well. Arman says he loves Maya but is really after her wealth. They have a brief courtship and there's a dance." Salman grinned at Maya. "You know what *that* means."

"I'm going to dance in the rain in a sari and get soaking wet," said Maya promptly.

They all cracked up—except for Natalie.

"You got it. I'll teach you a few steps and send you a link with a tutorial," said Salman. "It'll be a brief sequence because we have to keep the movie under thirty minutes."

"I'll out-dance Sridevi and Karishma Kapoor combined," said Maya, giggling.

Spoken like a true Bollywood fan. Salman was amazed she even remembered the names of the actors. Eye roll from Natalie. Smiles from the rest. That was all that mattered to Salman. He continued.

"When Arman kidnaps Maya for ransom—a plan hatched by Arman and Natalie—Jason and I rescue Maya after an impressive fight with the villains," Salman continued. "Arman, Natalie and the gang are arrested, charged, and sent to jail. Maya's father is so grateful for the boys' heroic act in rescuing his daughter that he rewards them with their own photography studio. They all become the best of friends and live happily ever after."

"Do I get to smash something?" asked Arman.

"You bet!" said Salman.

"I don't even know how to *walk* in a sari let alone dance!" said Maya, suddenly. "I'm going to trip and fall."

That set off Jason and Arman. The boys rolled on the floor, laughing.

"Stop it, you two," said Maya sternly, but she was smiling.

"You'll be fine, Maya," said Salman. "We'll let you practice first."

Ramesh quietly left the room.

Salman locked eyes with Natalie. Her face was pale. Her dark eyes shone in the soft lighting of the media room.

"So?" he asked, heart thudding.

"No," she said. "Absolutely not."

Chapter Six

The boys stopped laughing. Jason wiped his eyes with the back of his hand. Arman stuffed a couple of potato chips into his mouth. Maya stared at Natalie.

Salman set down the paper on the table and took a sip of warm soda. "Why not?"

"It's illogical," said Natalie. "Too many plot holes, and the end is too neat. Life isn't like that."

"What do the rest of you say?" Salman asked. "I thought it would be fun. This movie has the entire emotional spectrum. We can use a minute or two of song from the movie by the same name that was released in 2008. As long as we're not making money off of it, there won't be any copyright issues. I checked."

"Natalie has a point," said Arman. "It sounds like fun, but it's kind of weird too. It's one thing *seeing* a movie. It's another to *be* in it."

"I have a ton of questions," said Jason. "Like, why doesn't Maya realize that Arman is after her money? And how do two gay photographers overpower a gang of bad guys who are probably experts at combat?"

"It's a *movie*," said Salman. He stood up and paced around the room. "Ms. Lopez will *love* the fact that this project includes action and diversity."

"Yeah," said Maya. "That it does."

"I have the cameras and lights and we can shoot it here on the weekend," said Salman. "I also have the software for post-production editing. It will mean hours of extra work, but I'm willing to do it. You all just have to show up for the filming and follow the script. Okay?"

His friends looked at each other. Natalie folded her arms across her chest. It was clear by her posture that her answer was no.

"Would it help if I showed you a Bollywood movie right now, Natalie?" asked Salman. "You can see for yourself how much fun it is."

"No thanks," said Natalie. "If this outline is anything to go by, I do not think I would like it."

"Please, everyone, can you at least give this a shot?" said Salman. "If anyone has better ideas, let's hear them. But we want our project to stand out. Right?"

"This is so weird, it *will* stand out," said Natalie.

"Stop being so negative," Salman snapped. "And anyway, you're outnumbered, four to one. Everyone else is on board, right?"

Arman exchanged a glance with Jason. They both looked at Maya. She nodded, and they turned to Salman. "We're in!"

Ramesh walked past the media room. Salman noticed him, but he was focused on Natalie. Everyone was now waiting for her answer. She looked at her hands, tucked her hair behind her ears. Untucked it again. Finally, she mumbled a single word. "Okay."

After everyone had left, Salman got to work on the script, tweaking the scenes and writing dialogue. Much later, he heard a light knock on the door.

"Come in," he called out.

Ramesh walked in with two cups of hot chocolate. He handed one to Salman. He perched on the edge of the bed and sipped from the other.

"You've done a lot of hard work," he said, jerking his chin at the pages strewn over the bed. "In a very short time. That's excellent."

"Thanks," said Salman. "They all laughed at my idea, but at least they agreed to do it. When they see the finished product and we get a standing ovation in class, they'll thank me properly. This is going to be a mega-hit!"

"You think so?" said Ramesh.

"Why, don't you?" said Salman.

"Bollywood movies are fun to watch if you understand *who* they're made for and *why*. Not all plots or themes are fair, even though they're very entertaining." Ramesh sipped his hot chocolate, watching Salman. "And your audience will be full of smart young people who want to change the world. Not to mention your cast. Do you think *they* think your script is fair?"

Salman leaned back against the pillows and took a gulp of hot chocolate. It was *really* hot and he scalded his tongue. He blew out, trying to cool his mouth. "*I* think it's fair," he replied. "Everyone has enough screen time. But the good guys have to win, so Jason and I will have a bit more than the others."

"That's not what I mean, and on some level, you know it. Natalie didn't like the script at all. Why do you think that is?"

"What did *you* think of it?" asked Salman, trying to change the direction of the conversation.

"The key problem is that the characters don't change or learn anything from their mistakes," said Ramesh. "You need to show your characters' growth. If you're not sure how to do that, why not ask your friends to help you? That's one way to make them feel a part of the project. Five heads are better than one." Ramesh gave Salman an encouraging smile.

"But this is *my* project," said Salman, sitting up straight. "*I'm* the producer, director and scriptwriter.

My friends don't know the *first* thing about writing a Bollywood script." He glared at Ramesh. Why couldn't he understand how important this was to Salman? No way was he going to mess up his script with silly suggestions. After all, he'd watched hundreds of movies. *He* was the expert.

"You'd still be the lead writer," said Ramesh. "You're only asking them to contribute ideas to make the script stronger. It's flat at the moment and, as Natalie said, ends too neatly. Life's *not* like that. You know that."

Annoyed, Salman let out a huge yawn. "I'm tired and it's a school night."

Ramesh stood up and took Salman's cup of half-finished chocolate from him. "Think about what I said," he said as he walked out the door. "I think together with your friends you could make a good film. Good night, Salman."

Salman didn't reply.

Chapter Seven

Early on Saturday morning, everyone gathered
at Salman's house for the shoot. They started
with a hot breakfast of scrambled eggs, toast,
sausages and baked beans. There was tea, coffee
and freshly squeezed orange juice. Salman had
told Ramesh he wanted it to be like a real film set,
with great catering and craft services. Ramesh,
as usual, came through.

But Salman was too excited to eat. "We're bringing in someone to do the makeup. Ramesh and I will take turns working the camera, depending on who is in the shot. When we're both in it, I'll set it up and start the recording with a remote device. If I'm not happy, there *will* be multiple takes. You will all have to be patient if we're going to make a great movie. Got it?"

"You're talking way too much for this early in the morning," said Jason, chewing his sausage and egg.

"Yeah, please shut up until we've finished eating and woken up properly," said Arman.

Maya frowned at her phone, a piece of toast inches away from her mouth. "Oh no," she said. "Weather app says it's going to rain all day."

"Every Bollywood movie has a dance sequence in the rain," said Salman. "I would have had to turn on the sprinkler system, but now nature will provide the real thing. Brilliant, isn't it?"

Maya took a nibble of her toast, looking dismayed. "I thought you were joking about dancing in the rain. Am I still wearing your mom's sari?"

"Yup!" said Salman. "And no, I wasn't joking."

Natalie sniggered, then went back to sipping coffee and scrolling through her phone.

"But it'll be cold and wet," said Maya. "Can't I do the shot in my jeans and T-shirt? And a rain jacket? At least I'll be dry."

"*Come on*, Maya, we have to get this right," said Salman, trying not to let his annoyance show. "You're behaving like you'll melt in the rain. It'll only be a few minutes, if we get it right. Most of the other shots are indoors. I've worked very hard on this and we only have this weekend to shoot. Don't forget that I need time to edit the footage too, before we present."

"Okay, okay," said Jason, gulping down the last of his juice. "We're all on board and in your hands, Mr. Director."

Salman tried not to grin, but his mouth curved into a smile anyway. *Bollywood, here I come.*

It grew darker and thunder rumbled across the sky. Salman had them run through the script a few times and each time it was better. Ramesh had only a few lines, which he'd already memorized. He was now helping the others by prompting them. Ramesh's friend Queenie, from a couple of houses down the street, arrived with her makeup box just as they ran through the story one last time.

"Who's first for makeup?" she asked, coming into the dining room.

"Maya is," said Salman, pointing to her. "We're shooting the love scene with Arman, in the rain. Let's get the dance sequence out of the way. Then we focus on the fight scenes and the ones with the dialogue." He'd thought it all out based on the natural lighting. Since daylight faded by about four in the afternoon, he wanted all the outdoor shots done by then. They could focus on the indoor ones later in the day and keep going till he had the raw footage he needed.

"See you later," said Maya as she hurried out of the dining room behind Queenie.

It turned out that Queenie was also the costume department. She would help them all get dressed, especially draping the sari for Maya.

"Natalie, you're next," said Salman. "Jason, Arman, get dressed and come to my room. I'll take care of our makeup."

"Whoa there, mister," said Jason. "I'm not putting on makeup." He looked so horrified, Salman had to bite the inside of his cheek to stop from laughing.

"You have to, or you'll look flat and colorless on-screen," said Salman. "Even male TV anchors put on makeup to read the news."

"No. Way," said Jason, crossing his hands over his chest. "This is for school and I'm not putting on makeup."

"What Jason said," Arman said. "We'll be the laughingstock of the class if they see us in makeup. You try to make us and I'm out."

"*At last* someone is seeing the stupidity of this," said Natalie. "A ballet number would have been so much simpler. And we'd be filming it in a warm and dry studio, indoors."

Salman glared at her. Here he was running around doing more than his share of the project. The only thing his friends had to do was go along with the plan, but all they did was whine and moan. When this was a hit with the class, they would all thank him. He might even have the rest of the class clamoring to be in his future productions, not to mention their project getting the best grade.

Maybe then his parents would think of spending more time with their talented son instead of jetting around the world, making deals.

He pushed the thought away. Time to focus.

Chapter Eight

Salman fiddled with the camera as he waited for Maya to appear. Arman had agreed to the lightest of makeup and was ready for his dance number. He was wearing dress pants, a bright red shirt and a black jacket.

It was pouring outside. The beech trees on the lawn swayed in the breeze. Salman couldn't have asked for a better setting. He turned on every single light. A haze of rain softened the glow of the outdoor lamps. *Perfect!* Once he adjusted the lighting in post-production and added the soundtrack, it would be so romantic. He hadn't spent hours on YouTube tutorials for *nothing*.

Maya walked into the kitchen in a bright pink sari. Queenie had done a good job with her hair and makeup. Salman stared at her. He'd never realized Maya was so pretty.

"How do I look?" she asked, twirling and almost face-planting. "Walking in a sari feels like wading through ankle deep water." She wobbled on her heels, hands on her hips, striking a dramatic pose.

"Cool!" said Jason and Arman in unison.

"Like a Bollywood star," said Salman.

"Like someone trying too hard to attract the wrong kind of attention," said Natalie. She entered the kitchen dressed in a red kurta over black leggings and slingback pumps. "As do I. Normal people don't dress like this. Why can't we make this movie more realistic?"

Natalie looked beautiful too, but Salman refused to compliment her. He prayed to every god his mom had ever mentioned for patience. A good director had to deal with the tantrums of stars. A blockbuster was worth this pain!

"Time to roll the camera," said Salman. "Ramesh! Join us, please."

They all gathered around the kitchen table, where Salman had laid out a hand-drawn diagram of the grounds. "Maya," said Salman. "Ramesh will have the music playing on the outdoor speakers while you and Arman dance. The dance sequence will only be a minute long in the movie, but I'll be taking at least three to four minutes of footage. That way I can select the best parts. Okay?"

Maya fiddled with the end of the sari, which hung over her shoulder all the way to the backs of her knees. "Sure," she said.

Salman ran a finger over the diagram. "You will run from this tree and up the slope where you will be on high ground—I want a shot of you outlined against the sky. Then you race to this tree here, into Arman's waiting arms. Then you dance in unison and we cut. Did you practice the moves from that link I sent you?"

"Yeah," said Maya, shooting a nervous glance out the window. She wrapped the sari around her bare arms as she shivered. "Can we get this over with? I'm already cold."

"Couldn't Maya and Arman fall in love over a coffee or a dinner date?" asked Natalie. "Same result, only more realistic and less uncomfortable. Why does it have to be a dance in the rain?"

Salman closed his eyes and counted to ten. When he opened them again, they were all staring at him. He sighed. Here they were, shooting a movie about friends, with a title that translated to "friendship." But none of them looked very friendly at the moment.

"Cue the music, Ramesh." Salman zipped up his jacket and lifted the video camera, covered in plastic, onto his shoulder.

Maya stood at the back door. She did not look happy. "Why does Arman get to dress in warm clothes but I get this flimsy sari and sleeveless blouse? It sucks."

Salman shrugged. "This is the Bollywood way. And so it is my way."

Music blared from the outdoor speakers. Maya stepped out into the pouring rain and gasped, hugging herself tightly. Arman was right behind her. He looked constipated.

"Let the rhythm of the music warm you!" said Salman, as he set up the shot. "Let it flow through you like blood. Feel the love, the heat."

Maya and Arman glared at him. They were not feeling the love or the warmth.

Salman moved a bit farther away. "ACTION!" he yelled.

Chapter Nine

Maya sneezed three times in a row. She and Arman were standing as near as they could to the space heater in the kitchen. Salman was examining the footage of the dance number.

"Bless you," said Salman, not taking his eyes off the video camera's screen.

"I'm freezing!" Maya said.

"Me too," said Arman as he dripped onto a mat. "I hate this."

"What are *you* griping about?" snapped Maya. "At least you're wearing more clothes."

"Which are just as wet as yours," Arman snapped back, toweling his face and hair. "I think Natalie has a point. We could just as easily have this romance play out over dinner."

"See this here," said Salman, pointing to the video screen. "Instead of looking into the camera while you shimmied, you were looking at the ground. The audience needs to see your love for Arman. Almost there, Maya. You nail this and we'll move on to the next scene. Arman, a bit more bounce in that booty please. You're way too rigid. Let's go, people!"

"Forget it!" said Maya through chattering teeth. "We've been out there for two hours already. I'm so cold I can barely feel my fingers and toes.

Your mom's sari is ruined, and if I step out into the rain once more, I'll freeze to death. I need a hot shower. If you say one more word, Sal, I'll tie you up in this sari, push you outside, and lock the door!"

"I'll help you, Maya," said Arman, his face patchy where he'd scrubbed off the makeup. "Enough is enough, Sal."

They both looked so fierce, Salman took a step back. "All right, fine. I'll make do with the footage we have. But just to let you know, some song sequences take *days* to film and we're not even close—" He stopped talking as Arman advanced on him, hands clenched into fists.

Natalie snorted.

Maya sneezed again.

Jason hurried over with a mug of steaming masala chai. "You okay? You're not looking too hot."

"Try frozen," said Maya, wrapping her hands around the mug and pressing it to her cheek.

Her fingernails were blue. "I'm going to change. Be right back." She hurried away, still sneezing.

"We're wasting time," said Salman. "Let's do the fight scene in the garage, where we have to rescue Maya from Arman and his gang. Ramesh has moved the cars out and I've improvised to make it look like an industrial warehouse. I'll CGI the rest."

"You do realize we don't have enough people, right?" said Arman. "Who are we fighting?"

As if on cue, the doorbell rang. Ramesh excused himself. Salman studied the script as the sounds of excited voices floated into the kitchen. Within minutes Ramesh returned. Three boys followed him into the kitchen.

"Hey, Salman," they all said at the same time.

Salman bumped fists with them and then introduced them. "Jason, Arman and Natalie, meet Josh, Roman and Piko. They live in the neighborhood and are excited to be in the movie."

"You bet," said Piko.

The other two just smiled. Salman sent them off to Queenie for makeup. They didn't protest. Salman had promised to pay them fifty bucks each to play a part in the movie, no questions asked.

"You *have* put in a lot of effort," said Natalie in a quiet voice. "I'll give you that. If only it were a more logical plot, more current, it really would be, what do you call it—a blockbuster."

Salman was surprised. But before he could reply, Maya returned. She was wearing denim shorts and a T-shirt tied at the waist. She looked much better, although still a little pale.

"Hey, Maya," said Salman. "Feeling better?"

She sneezed in response and poured herself another warm drink. Ramesh had put out a bunch of snacks and thermoses of tea and hot chocolate.

"Let's get on with it, yeah?" She sounded a lot less enthusiastic than before. "I want to go home and crawl under the covers. I'm still freezing."

They gathered around the kitchen table as Salman explained the fight sequence. "Arman, you will let the others do the dirty work while you have a tight hold on Maya, who is struggling to free herself."

"Natalie, you're in love with Arman, which is why you agreed to this kidnapping. Look angry, but happy, very much in love, yet a bit anxious."

"How am I supposed to do *all* that?" said Natalie. "That's not normal."

"It's called acting," said Salman. "Watch me." He contorted his face to show the range of emotions he was looking for. "Now you try it."

Natalie rolled her eyes. "You look like you need to go the bathroom," she said. "I'm *not* doing that."

Everyone laughed, but one look from Salman silenced them. This was taking up so much energy. Why couldn't they just follow orders? Sheesh! He wanted to start yelling, to point out that *he* was the director, but he told himself that they would thank him later. Until then, he'd just have to do the best he could.

Natalie looked at her watch. "It's past noon already."

"Then we better get started," said Salman and led the way to the garage.

Chapter Ten

"More enthusiasm as you swing your fists," said Salman. "Deliver the dialogue ínto the camera. Scream a bit louder, Maya! Like you mean it. You're scared for your life."

They'd been filming all afternoon and still did not have the perfect footage. Someone or other flubbed lines or didn't deliver them to Salman's satisfaction. He made them re-take the shot.

Everyone's enthusiasm was dribbling away fast. Maya was just going through the motions. They were all such whiners.

Jason hobbled up to him. "I almost twisted my ankle jumping down from that crate. Why can't I stand here and fight? This is stupid and dangerous."

"If I can do it, so can you," said Salman. "Fight scenes are all about the stunts. Standing on the ground and punching away is boring."

"My throat's sore from yelling dialogue," said Natalie. "I'd be more believable if I spoke in a normal voice. Can we stop now? I've had enough."

Maya shivered in a parka that Arman had loaned her. The wind was picking up, finding its way through tiny cracks in the doorway, making the garage colder. They needed to shoot faster. Plus, the three "villains" he'd hired were costing him from his own allowance. This movie was already way over budget on the first day. This would never do.

Salman could not keep it in any longer.

"You're all such WIMPS!" he yelled. "*I'm* doing all the hard work, not to mention the prep that went into this shot and the hours of work that will come after. All you guys have to do is act and say a few lines, but all I'm hearing is whining."

"How can Maya not realize that her best friend hates her and her boyfriend is a scumbag?" said Natalie. "Especially when you have provided so many clues to the audience. I don't think your main character needs to be thick. Why not make her intelligent but have her fail because of events out of her control?"

"And why doesn't my dad call the police and track me down?" asked Maya, joining the argument. "And how is it that Jason and you can take on three guys, get so badly beaten up that blood's trickling down your faces, and you both still keep fighting? You should be in the hospital by now! If *I* don't buy this, the audience won't."

"A BOLLYWOOD BLOCKBUSTER IS ABOUT ENTERTAINMENT, NOT REALITY!" Salman cried. "The audience will suspend disbelief and get lost in a movie as long as it's fun and loud and entertaining. As long as it makes them feel every emotion under the sun. There's no 'ordinary' in a blockbuster. Bollywood churns out almost 200 movies a year. A multi-billion dollar industry knows what their audience wants!"

"That's not what our class, or Ms. Lopez, wants!" Natalie shouted back. "They're not watching a three-hour movie. It's a short film. Our story needs to make sense in a way that *our* audience can understand. I agreed to do it your way, Salman, but I did not agree to doing stupid things. I can tell you now, the class won't be entertained.

They'll be confused." She flung her script in the air and stomped toward the door. "I'm out."

The pages fluttered to the floor.

"Natalie, wait," said Salman. "Please, we have to finish this. We're running out of time."

Eyes blazing, Natalie whirled around. "Your Bollywood film industry is very weird. The guys get to dress decently while the girls wear flimsy saris, no matter what the weather. And why is it always the *girls* who need rescuing? Why not boys? This kind of storytelling is old-fashioned and one-sided. I want no part of it."

"You think Hollywood is any different?" said Salman. "Have you watched any American movies lately? At least Bollywood does not expect their heroines to shed their clothes at the drop of a hat."

"For once I agree with you," Natalie said, in a softer voice. "Don't you think it is time we changed the story? If this is the way it's *always* been done, it is up to us, artists of *this* generation, to do it differently. If you don't change it, you're basically saying you're agreeing with this way of thinking."

"Okay, how about you agree to stay and finish this?" said Salman. "And the next movie we make will be the way you all want it. Sound good?"

Natalie shook her head. "I'm sorry, but I'm asking Ms. Lopez to assign me to another group. I can't do this anymore. Maya? Are you staying or coming with me?"

Maya looked as if she wanted to bolt.

In fact, Salman realized, all his friends looked unhappy. "You guys feel the same way?" he asked, his voice a bit shaky. "I thought you loved the movies we watched. You knew what a Bollywood movie was, and you all agreed. Are you telling me you were lying?"

"Sorry, Sal," said Arman. "I'm with Natalie. I did want to support you. But I feel like a weirdo doing stuff that a normal person would not do. The script has to make *sense*, and Natalie is right. The message is important." He was sweating, and the makeup ran down his face in rivulets. It looked like he was melting.

"Are you going to abandon me too, Jason?" Salman asked.

Jason nodded, slipping off the jacket he'd been wearing and wiping his face. Piko, Josh, and Roman, who'd been staying in the background, started to fidget.

"You're making a huge mistake," Salman said. He meant to sound confident, but his heart wasn't really in it.

As she reached the garage door, Natalie turned and faced him. "You said the title of this story means *friendship*. Let me tell you, you don't understand the *first* thing about it. You're a lousy friend if you can't or won't understand what we're trying to tell you." Then she walked out. Maya, Arman, and Jason followed right behind her.

"You'll still pay us for today's work, won't you?" asked Piko.

"Ramesh will pay you," said Salman. "Now go."

"Should we come back tomorrow?" Roman asked.

"It's over," said Salman. "Please go."

Salman tried not to cry. Heroes didn't start bawling when things got tough. But then, he reminded himself, there was no movie and no hero. His debut production hadn't even made it through the first day of shooting.

His career was over before it had started. And so was their project.

Dostana was a flop in every sense.

Chapter Eleven

Salman sat in his room watching the raw footage of the movie. It wasn't all bad, especially for a first attempt. Why had he been so demanding? Why had he insisted his friends do the scene over and over, ignoring their suggestions or objections? Because he wanted to produce a good movie and get a good mark. That was all.

But was it?

There was a knock on the door. Salman knew it was Ramesh. He didn't answer. He wasn't in the mood for a lecture.

The door opened and Ramesh stepped in with two steaming mugs of hot chocolate. "Are you okay?" he said, setting down the mugs on Salman's desk. "You barely ate anything during dinner."

"No," said Salman. "Please leave me alone."

"Can't do that," said Ramesh. He took his usual spot on the edge of the bed. He calmly sipped his chocolate and stared out the window. Rain slid down the window in rivulets, blurring the world outside.

Salman reached for his mug and wrapped his hands around it. He inhaled the creamy fragrance. Took a sip. The sweet, hot liquid shot down his throat and into his stomach. He realized he was starving.

"What did I do wrong?" he asked Ramesh, staring at his reflection in the dark window.

There was a long silence, and Salman wondered if Ramesh was mad at him too. But then Ramesh spoke. "You tried to do it all on your own, Salman. For any project to be successful, you need teamwork. Even a marriage depends on teamwork. Ask your mom and dad."

Thinking about his parents brought a whole other kind of pain, so Salman focused on his friends and the project.

"They were all in the movie and *everyone* had a good role," said Salman. "Don't forget, *I* did all the work. *I* wrote the script. *I* set up the shots and gave them all direction. *I* hired the extras. And *I* offered my place to shoot it. Then *I* was going to spend hours on post-production."

Ramesh tore his gaze away from the window and looked at him. "You used the word *I* six times just now. Not once did I hear a *we*."

Salman slumped back in his chair as Ramesh's words sunk in. This was supposed to be a group project, and he'd completely taken over. His friends, his *wonderful* friends, had gone along with it as far as they could. But then he'd gone from demanding to unbearable and they'd given up and left.

"I've been an idiot, haven't I?" Salman put his mug on the table and held his head in his hands. "What am I going to do?"

"We all make mistakes," said Ramesh. His eyes were kind and his voice soft. "In fact, our mistakes are the *best* way we learn and grow. Goodness knows I've made quite a few in my lifetime. But the important thing is to set them right if you can. Each of us has the power to do that."

Salman watched Ramesh. How had he never realized that he was so much more than the guy who drove him around and cooked his meals? Ramesh was an intelligent, kind man who cared for him. Salman thought back to all the things Ramesh did—quietly, efficiently, to make Salman feel better without ever demanding credit for it. They, too, were a team, and it worked because they consulted each other on most things.

"What should I do?" asked Salman. "The weekend is almost over. I doubt any of them would be willing to come back tomorrow to reshoot. Presentations are due this week. It will be my fault if we fail. They'll hate me even more."

"I'm sure you'll figure it out. Whatever you decide, I will help you," said Ramesh. "But only *you* can make this right. Maybe you start with something as simple as saying you're sorry. Maybe then the solution will become clear."

"Yeah, maybe you're right, Ramesh. Thank you."

"Good night, Salman."

"Good night," Salman replied.

Sleep was a very long time coming for Salman that night.

Chapter Twelve

It was tough getting out of bed on Monday. Salman had thought about nothing but the project for the rest of the weekend. Not one of his friends had texted or called him. What if no one wanted to speak to him ever again? The more he thought about it, the more he realized that *he* had been the only one behaving badly. Natalie had made some good comments about the script. He knew that now. And his friends had done their best to stick by him. He was the one who had made it impossible. He had to figure out a way to apologize. But what if they refused to speak to him?

Ramesh dropped him off at school as always. Before he drove away, he rolled down the window. "Be honest with your friends and they will forgive you."

Salman nodded, trying not to let his irritation show. It was so easy to give advice and so hard to follow it. But he knew it was the first step if he wanted to salvage the project. He'd have to go through with it, no matter how hard it was. But he had one important thing he had to do first. He hurried inside, searching for the one person he needed to speak to right away.

The corridors were busy. Students took books out of their lockers and tried to cram bags and jackets into the narrow spaces. Salman raced for the staff room. He wanted to catch Ms. Lopez before she headed to class.

When he got there, he saw something that made him stop suddenly. A girl behind him bumped right into him.

"Sorry," she said, as he turned around to apologize to her. They gave each other sheepish smiles. She hurried away and Salman ducked into a corner where he could watch the staff-room door.

Natalie was already chatting with Ms. Lopez. Her arms were flying and Ms. Lopez was shaking her head. Salman's face burned. There was no doubt in his mind that Natalie was talking about him and their project. He'd hoped to get to Ms. Lopez first, but Natalie had beat him to it. *She* was the one who had started the complaining, and the others had followed. He started to feel annoyed but squashed the feeling down. No. He needed to own this. If *he* hadn't been so pigheaded and forced them all to do things his way, none of this would have happened.

The warning bell for the start of school buzzed through the halls. He waited and watched, wishing Natalie would hurry up. Ms. Lopez's expression was serious. She said something and then left the staff room. Natalie stared at the teacher's receding back with a frown. Then she left too and hurried to class. Salman followed, staying a good distance behind. He did not want to talk to any of his friends until he'd spoken to Ms. Lopez.

Maya, Arman and Jason were by the window, whispering. They had not seen him come in. He desperately wanted to go over and talk to them, but his legs refused to move. What if they shut him out? No one had spoken to him since

Saturday night, which meant they were still mad at him. While he stood there, wondering what to do, their teacher walked in. Everyone took their seats. By now they must have seen him, but no one waved hi or smiled, even though he'd glanced at them several times. Was their friendship over for good?

The morning limped by and the bell for lunch sounded. Salman stuffed his books into his bag. Without looking at anyone, he raced out of the classroom. He had to get to Ms. Lopez, but he couldn't find her anywhere, not in the staff room, not on the grounds, not in the library. Time was running out for him and his group.

Salman shuffled into the cafeteria to grab a quick bite. And there was Ms. Lopez. Jason, Maya and Arman were crowded around her, talking excitedly.

Salman's heart zoomed to his toes, and his hunger evaporated. By now, his favorite teacher knew he was a jerk. He'd hoped to tell his side first, but it was too late now. Had she assigned them all to different groups, leaving him alone?

He was about to slink away when Ramesh's words echoed in his head. There was no harm in saying he was sorry. He was going to do it here and now, in front of everyone. He walked up to them. His friends had their backs to him and hadn't seen him approach, but Ms. Lopez did. She nodded at him and all three turned to look at him. Jason said a cool hello. Arman gave a small smile. Maya still looked angry.

"We'll talk to you later, Ms. Lopez—" Maya began, but Salman cut in.

"What I have to say concerns all my group members, so please stay," said Salman, looking around at them. "I want to say I'm sorry for taking over the project and not giving everyone a chance to contribute. It's my fault we weren't able to complete it this weekend."

"I appreciate your honesty, Salman," said Ms. Lopez. "And I would have been open to discuss this earlier. But your project is due on Wednesday. I cannot put you in new groups because the others will have completed the project, or at least done most of it by now. You'll have to come up with something else or accept a failing mark. I'm sorry."

Salman glanced at his friends. They had trusted and followed him, and he'd let them down. But he was going to set it right and now came the most important part of his plan. He had his fingers crossed. "Would you give us the long weekend to work on the project? We'll be ready on Monday. Please, Ms. Lopez, I'd—we'd like the chance to make this work. Right, guys?"

No one answered him.

Ms. Lopez looked around the group and then back at Salman. "I could do that, but I will have to deduct a few points for the extra time. I need to be fair to those who turn in the project on time. Are you all willing to take a deduction?"

Salman gazed round at the group, his heart beating so hard, he could barely hear the usual noise in the cafeteria. Maya looked at Jason, then Arman. She stared at Salman briefly and then nodded.

"Yes, Ms. Lopez. We'll have to check with Natalie, but I think we can all work together and get this done."

Salman swallowed the lump in his throat.

Chapter Thirteen

After Ms. Lopez left, Salman turned to his friends. "Thank you for agreeing to this. Again, I'm sorry for being such an ass. Especially to you, Maya. How are you?"

"I spent all of yesterday in bed, but I'm better now," she said with a shrug.

She still looked peaky. Had he really made her stay outdoors in freezing rain in a skimpy outfit for almost two hours? The thought made him cringe. Even though Arman had been soaked to the skin too, at least he'd been less exposed to the wind. The others were watching him, so he spoke up.

"How's your foot?" he asked Jason.

"Okay," said Jason.

They stood around awkwardly.

"I have to talk to Natalie," said Salman. "Can you all meet me at the main entrance after school today? We'll head to my place for dinner and figure this out. Okay?" His voice wobbled, and he looked at the floor. He was trying very hard not to cry.

Suddenly Jason slung an arm around him. "Water under the bridge. Let's move on."

"You all forgive me?" Salman asked.

"Sure," said Arman, slapping him on the back. "That was smart, to ask for extra time. But what are we going to do?"

"I have an idea. I'll tell you later and then you can tell me what you think. Or if you have a better plan, we'll discuss it. Thanks again for agreeing to finish this," said Salman. The gloom had lifted and he was feeling hopeful again. Excited, even.

Jason fist-bumped him, and Maya smiled. Salman could tell it was genuine because the smile reached her eyes.

For the rest of lunch, Salman raced around the school looking for Natalie, but she seemed to have vanished. He knew he could catch her in one of his afternoon classes though. It was with a lighter heart that he entered his last class. Sure enough, Natalie was seated in the front row. She did not look anywhere but straight ahead. Salman thought of passing her a note, but if she was still mad at him, she'd hand it straight to the teacher. Detention was the last thing he needed this week. He made himself wait. It felt like walking on burning coals.

He'd got *three* members of the group to agree to his plan. The toughest one was coming up, but he'd manage it. He was already bubbling over with things he would tell her and how they could rewrite the script together over the next two days and then shoot it.

"Salman, I asked you a question," said the teacher.

"I'm sorry, Miss," said Salman. "Could you please repeat it?"

He earned a glare and a warning, but it didn't bother him one bit. Finally the bell rang. Students poured out into the hallway, chattering and pulling on their jackets as they headed outside. Natalie had zipped out ahead of him and disappeared in the crowd. Salman grabbed his things from his locker and pushed his way to the main entrance, praying the others would be there.

Thankfully, Maya had snagged Natalie and was chatting with her. Jason and Arman were there too. Before his nerve failed him, he hurried up to them.

"Hi, Natalie," said Salman.

Natalie's look was cold. "What do you want?" she said.

"To apologize for my behavior," said Salman. "I was an idiot, and I'm sorry. These three," he said, flicking his eyes around the group, "have already forgiven me. If you're on board, we can finish this project."

"Are we still doing the Bollywood movie?" she asked, staring at the rest of the group.

"Yes," said Salman, "but this time, we're *all* going to pitch in to write the script. It will be fun, current, and most important—it will make sense." He grinned.

"Do we even have the time?" Natalie asked, frowning. "It's due in two days! There's no way this will work."

"Genius here already took care of that," said Jason, nudging Salman. "Tell her."

"I bought us some extra time," said Salman, trying not to sound annoyed. He had messed up, and she had a right to know how they would pull it off. He'd always known she would be the toughest one to convince. "I spoke to Ms. Lopez. She said we could have the long weekend to prepare, and present on Monday."

"What's the catch?" said Natalie. "There has to be one."

She was smart, thought Salman. If he wasn't so annoyed with her, he'd totally be into her.

"Ms. Lopez will dock a few points, in fairness to the rest of the class," said Salman. "But our movie is going to be so fantastic, we'll still get a good—no a *great* mark. So, are you in?"

The crowds streaming past them had thinned. A cold wind shook the trees. Salman zipped up his jacket and stuck his hands into his pockets. What if someone told him he had to spend two hours in shorts and a T-shirt, right this minute? The thought was enough to give him goosebumps. How had Maya done it? A fresh wave of shame washed over him. Respect too, for how sporting she'd been.

Natalie studied each of their faces. Her eyes came to rest on Salman. How had he not noticed that her eyes were bright and intelligent? And the way she wrinkled her nose when she was deep in thought was cute.

"No thanks," Natalie said. "I asked Ms. Lopez if I could do a solo project and she agreed. She said she'd dock a point or two because this was supposed to be a group project and I agreed. Sorry, but I have to run. Lots to do."

She tried to side-step Salman, but he stood firm. "Please, Natalie, we need you for our movie. I think you'd be amazing. Okay, I made a mistake, and I'm apologizing. Everyone deserves a second chance. Come with us—we're headed to my place. We'll have dinner and crack that script tonight."

Natalie gave him the coldest glare ever. "I've made up my mind, and once I do, I *never* change it. It's a waste of time and very inefficient. Please get out of my way."

Salman stepped aside. Luckily, he wasn't cold anymore. He was burning up with anger at Natalie's pig-headed behavior.

Chapter Fourteen

Ramesh had prepared tandoori chicken, naan, daal, and rice for dinner. The group, ravenous after a long day, had stuffed themselves. Now they all sat in the media room with pencils and copies of the script in hand. Salman looked around the room and his heart glowed.

Jason was so relaxed, he was almost horizontal on the floor. Arman sat close to the snacks and

Maya was curled up on the couch with her favorite pillow. They were all where they should be. There was only one person absent and, surprisingly, Salman missed her. But there was nothing he could do. Best get on with it.

"Shall we begin?" asked Salman.

"You bet," said Maya. "I was thinking we should make this a rom-com—a romantic comedy. Even if we don't have Natalie, I can ask one of my friends to help."

"Sounds good," said Jason.

"What's the plot?" said Arman. "Nothing outdoors, please. I'm not shooting outside in this miserable weather. There's going to be rain all week, including the weekend."

"It will be indoors," said Salman. "You have my word."

The doorbell chimed. A bit late for a delivery, thought Salman. He heard Ramesh hurry to the door.

"I quite like the bit where you and I are pretending to be gay to rent an apartment with Maya," said Jason. "That part has potential for comedy and should stay."

At the sound of footsteps, they all looked up. Natalie stood in the doorway, her back rigid, her smile sheepish. "My solo project wasn't fun so I changed my mind. You still want me in the group?"

Maya threw the pillow into the air, jumped up and hugged her. Jason and Arman gave her a thumbs-up, though neither moved an inch from their spots.

"I'm thrilled that you changed your mind," said Salman. "We need you."

Natalie smiled, walked in and plunked herself down beside him. "So, where are we?"

"Have you eaten?" asked Ramesh from the doorway. "Would you like me to get you something?"

Natalie thanked him but said she'd already eaten. They all got to work.

"You can share my script," said Salman. "Or I could go print a copy for you."

"Let's share," said Natalie.

Over the next two hours, they worked on the script, on the dialogue and, most important, the plot.

"So a main difference from the original script is that even though Salman and Jason fall in love with Maya, she doesn't pay attention to either of them," said Salman. "Then what?"

"What if we give Maya a different love interest?" Natalie suggested. "What if she's interested in a *girl*—me!"

"Genius!" said Salman.

There was a chorus of yeses, and Natalie blushed a deep pink.

"Let's talk this through," said Salman. "How do Natalie and Maya meet?"

"Me!" said Arman. "I'm Maya's best friend. I introduce her to Natalie, and they fall in love. We can have each boy take Maya out on a date to woo her, and it falls flat because she's just not interested."

"How about a scene where Jason takes her to an art show, and Salman whisks her away through the back door to another venue?" said Natalie.

"Or I take her to a fancy restaurant and Jason bribes the server to deliver over-spiced food, which ruins the evening," said Salman.

"And Maya says, 'Is this a date or a torture session? I surrender!'" said Natalie with a laugh.

Back and forth they went, tweaking the original plot. Watching them, Salman realized how much more fun this was. Plus, the script was so much better than he could ever have come up with alone. They'd be able to shoot this in a day.

Ramesh arrived with masala chai and samosas. They helped themselves to the snacks as they continued to work. By ten in the evening, they had a script that everyone, especially Salman, was happy with.

"Natalie, why don't you read out the changes?" said Salman. "I'll type them up tomorrow and give you all the revised script with the dialogue."

Natalie gave him a warm smile, cleared her throat and started reading.

"*Friends and struggling photography artists (Jason and Salman) need to rent an apartment in a city, but the only room available is with a girl (Maya) whose father (Ramesh) will not allow it. They pretend to be gay (because the room is really nice and affordable) and convince Maya and Ramesh that they are harmless because they have no interest in their daughter. They're in love with each other. At first Ramesh is very old-fashioned* and is not on board with the gay couple, but Maya convinces him to give them a chance.

"Unfortunately, both Salman and Jason fall in love with their roommate and try to sabotage the other's chances with her. Their ploys include a bad restaurant date and a disappearance at an art show.

"Maya meets Natalie through her friend Arman and falls for her. The feelings are returned. In the meantime, the boys are still trying to woo Maya, not realizing her affections lie elsewhere.

"When Maya's father decides that it is time she got married and tries to invite suitable boys over so he can arrange a match, Maya confesses that she's in love with Natalie and they might even decide to marry. Her father is outraged, and now the boys step in to help Maya out. They explain to Ramesh that this is the way it is. If he forces Maya into marriage, he will ruin her life and happiness. She will never forgive him for that.

"*Ramesh finally sees that acceptance is the best course of action and gives Maya and Natalie his blessing. He suggests a double wedding for Maya and Natalie and Salman and Jason, whom he now considers part of the family.*

"*Salman and Jason are caught in their lie and confess that they're not really gay but had to pretend to get the apartment. It's a hilarious reversal of roles. Their lie is forgiven and all four live harmoniously in the apartment, becoming better friends than ever.*"

"I love it, yeah!" said Maya.

"Ditto," said Jason.

Arman gave a thumbs-up sign because his mouth was full of samosa.

Salman looked at Natalie. "Welcome to the Bollywood club."

She grinned. "This will be fun now, with the new script."

"And no dancing in the rain!" Maya added.

Salman looked at his hands, trying not to ruin the jubilant mood. All Bollywood movies had *one* song at least. Sometimes the songs became blockbusters in their own right. There were remixes, dance-offs and fan videos based on the original. A song in a Hindi movie was like the salt in a recipe. The dish could have the *best* flavors, but skip the salt and it was incomplete. *But* the group had decided against a song, and there was no way he would make the mistake of forcing them to include one.

"There's one last thing we need to agree on," said Natalie. "Come here so I can show you."

Everyone crowded around Natalie as she unlocked her phone.

"I saw a video on YouTube for this song 'Ghungroo,' from the Hindi movie *War*."

"You watched that movie?" Salman was shocked.

Natalie smiled. "I like to do a lot of research before I start a project."

"Well, this song was a mega-hit!" said Salman.

"I'll say," said Jason. "Two hundred and ninety *million* views."

"Yeah, well, I found this channel where a couple of women teach the steps to the dance. I thought we could study it and do a short clip, right at the end of the movie. End on a fun and high note with all four characters celebrating their friendship. It's a great workout too," she added.

"I don't know…" said Maya, looking serious.

Salman was worried. If she refused, there would be no convincing the others.

Natalie managed to get the YouTube channel up onto the big screen. As soon as it was over, Maya turned to them, her eyes shining. "Yeah! I'm totally on board. I could barely stop my feet. The class will go wild!"

They watched it again and tried a few steps. It was much harder than it looked. But they agreed it was going to be worth it.

Ramesh interrupted them by coming into the room. "Time to call it a day, everyone. It's late. I'll drop you all home."

Salman waved goodbye to his friends and sat down at the computer right away, making changes, laughing at certain bits of dialogue they'd all contributed to. He was thrilled that Natalie had suggested the dance number. It was the final touch. If only he'd done this right at the start, they might have shot the movie on time, and earned a super mark with no points docked. He'd been an idiot. But it was all going to work out, like things always did in the best Bollywood movies.

Salman printed out the revised script of *Dostana* and tucked it under his pillow. He fell asleep quickly and did not wake up till the next morning.

Chapter Fifteen

Salman rubbed his tired eyes as he stared at the screen. He'd been working on the post-production editing all day and needed a break. He wandered down to the media room and flopped onto the couch. They'd finished shooting yesterday, despite the many re-takes. The short dance sequence had been tough to do, but so much fun. Even Natalie had said she'd never had such a rigorous workout as learning to do a Bollywood number. Dancing to "Ghungroo" required agility, excellent timing, stamina and style. The catchy beat had made the effort worthwhile.

That was yesterday, and the house had been full. Tonight Salman's friends were all with their respective families, spending some quality time together. Salman sat in the darkness, staring out the window as evening turned to night. His parents had been delayed yet again and apologized for not making it home at all this weekend.

Ramesh walked by the media room. He stopped and came back inside.

"What's the matter?" he asked, switching on the light.

Salman shrugged. "I wish Mom and Dad were here. Thanksgiving doesn't feel the same without them."

Ramesh sat down beside him. "I know you miss them a lot. I'm sure they miss you too. But think of all the things you already have: your health, a good home, a very comfortable lifestyle and great friends who love you. Isn't that quite a lot to be thankful for?"

Salman stared into Ramesh's eyes. Ramesh wasn't much older than Dad, but he seemed very, very wise. Salman felt a lot better when he thought about all the things he *did* have, rather than the things that were missing.

"Ready for our own Thanksgiving dinner?" Ramesh asked. "I know it is usually celebrated on the Thursday, but I felt like creating a feast tonight."

"You hate turkey," said Salman, surprised. But then he realized Ramesh must have done this to make him feel better about his parents being away. "So do I."

"I made Cornish hens with garam masala to go with spicy potatoes."

Salman laughed. "I'm in. Lead the way."

Ramesh's friend Queenie joined them as well. She'd brought homemade rasmalai. The three of them shared a non-traditional Thanksgiving meal that Salman thought was perfect. He complimented both Ramesh and Queenie.

After dinner, Salman sat at his computer in a much better mood. He did not plan to get up till he'd finished the editing. Since the next day was Sunday, he could work as late as he liked.

He watched the raw footage. They'd shot all of it indoors and no one had been uncomfortable or cold. Outside, the wind gusted and rain pattered against the window. Much as he loved Bollywood movies, he realized that some aspects of it were silly. Natalie had been right. What couple in love would choose to run around in the icy rain when they could snuggle indoors, warm and cozy?

For the restaurant scene, he'd filmed a close-up of their own dinner table, with the rest of them in the back, out of focus. Arman, dressed as a server, had delivered their meal, which had been over-spiced, causing an uproar. They'd shot the art scene in the upstairs corridor where his parents had hung many beautiful paintings by famous artists. His house was large enough that they could film it in different places and make it seem like an entirely new location. They'd used his own bedroom as the room the boys rented.

At three in the morning, he finished. He sent a text to the group.

Dostana is ready. First viewing tomorrow at whatever time you can make it.

He did not expect a reply, but Jason texted back to say he was free around four o'clock. Salman texted a thumbs-up sign and fell into bed. He was asleep before his head touched the pillow.

Natalie was the last to arrive the next day. "Sorry I'm late, everyone. I missed the three-thirty bus."

"Don't worry about it," said Salman. "Ready?"

"Not without something to munch on," said Arman.

As if on cue, Ramesh arrived with masala chai and banana cake. They all settled in to watch *Dostana*. No one said a word throughout the movie. There was laughter during the funny parts, but other than that, total silence. The screen went black, and the credits rolled. Every one of them was listed, including Ramesh.

Salman looked at the group, his stomach churning. Why had they not commented on anything? Did they hate it? Salman looked at Natalie. She would be the first to express her disappointment, and the others would follow.

Natalie stood up and came over to Salman. Her expression was so serious, Salman's pulse raced. She reached out a hand and pulled him to his feet. Then she gave him a hug.

"That was *awesome!*" she said. "Thank you for sharing the producing credit with all of us, even though you did most of the work."

One by one his friends crowded around him, slapping him on the back, shaking his hand. Salman swallowed the lump in his throat as he caught Ramesh's eye. Ramesh smiled and slipped out of the room.

"Teamwork," Salman said.

"Dostana," said Natalie.

"To friendship!" said Maya, Jason and Arman at the same time, clinking their mugs.

Chapter Sixteen

Ms. Lopez had given them the last half hour of the last period of the day to show their project. The class was sluggish and sleepy after a long weekend of food and probably too little sleep. Not a good time to be showing a movie with the lights dimmed, but they had no choice.

Salman's stomach was in knots as he helped Ms. Lopez set up his laptop, which would project the movie onto the classroom's whiteboard. He'd been so sure that this was the way to go, but now, looking at the sleepy, disinterested faces around him, he was worried.

"It'll be okay," Natalie whispered when he took his seat again.

"Class," said Ms. Lopez, "the group made up of Natalie, Maya, Arman, Jason and Salman had a bit of a hiccup with their project. They asked for some extra time. But they have finished, and we're now going to see their project. Please give it your full attention."

There was a murmur of voices. "No fair. Why did they get extra time?"

Salman's heart sank. *Great. Not only were they sleepy and raring to go home, but now they'd be resentful too and would hate the movie before they even saw it.*

Ms. Lopez looked sternly around the room, and the chatter died away immediately. "You know that I am always fair. The group has agreed to my docking a few points for submitting this late. If any of you needed more time for your project, all you had to do was ask."

The silence in the class was answer enough.

"Let's watch this, and we can discuss it tomorrow," said Ms. Lopez. "Go ahead, Salman."

Salman pressed *play*, and the title credits came up. The catchy soundtrack started playing in the background. The students became more alert. All eyes were glued to the screen.

Salman glanced around the room. His classmates were upright in their seats. Some were drumming their fingers on their tables or swaying in time to the song's beat.

Yessss!

In what seemed like no time at all, the film was done. There were hoots and hollers at the dance sequence, and then the final credits rolled.

Salman hurried to the computer, turned it off and switched on the lights. Ms. Lopez stood up and started clapping. Almost everyone joined in.

"Good job, man!"

"Cool!"

"Amazing!"

"That was very well done," said Ms. Lopez. "A fun story with a nice twist at the end. You've given me a taste of Bollywood and now I feel like I *must* watch another one this weekend. I'll ask you for recommendations."

Salman grinned. "We all worked hard to finish this. Thanks for the extra time, Ms. Lopez."

The bell went off. Chairs scraped across the floor in unison as everyone headed for the door. Salman slipped his laptop into his bag as the rest of the group gathered around him.

"We pulled it off, yeah?" said Maya. She high-fived Salman.

"Yup," said Salman.

"Free for the weekend, *finally*," said Jason. "I'm going skiing."

"I have babysitting," said Maya. "And piano lessons."

"I have to help my dad with some project or other," said Arman with a frown.

"I enjoyed working with you all," said Natalie. "Wish we could make another one."

"There's a new Bollywood movie being released this Friday," said Salman. "It's called *Rahasya (The Secret)*. It's had great reviews. Um…anyone interested in coming over to watch?"

"Yes!" came the resounding reply from Maya, Arman and Jason.

Natalie tucked her arm in Salman's. "Wouldn't miss it for the world."

Author's Note

The songs for Bollywood movies, which have big budgets and are often shot in exotic places, are a huge part of the productions' success. The audiences have come to love and expect them. The movie *War* that Natalie and Salman talk about was released in 2019 and had a mega-hit song called "Ghunghroo." At the time of writing, the video has had 290 million views on YouTube. It has spawned many remixes, dances and fan videos.

BFUNK is a dance class created by Shivani Bhagwan and Chaya Kumar. Based in Los Angeles, the duo teaches a fusion of Bollywood and Bhangra moves with hip hop and jazz funk. Their choreography for "Ghungroo" has been watched on YouTube over 14 million times.

Acknowledgments

Thanks to Naomi Davis, my champion, friend and agent extraordinaire. A heartfelt thanks to Mom, who always believed that a good education was the key to success in life and who first instilled the love for reading in me. Thanks, as always, to Rahul and Aftab. You are my world. Finally, thanks to my brilliant editor, Tanya Trafford, who brings enthusiasm and sensitivity to every project we work on.

Mahtab Narsimhan is the award-winning author of several books for young readers, including *Embrace the Chicken*, *Mission Mumbai*, *The Tiffin* and *The Third Eye*, which won the Silver Birch Award. She was a Writer in Residence at the Toronto District School Board from 2015 to 2016. Born in Mumbai, Mahtab immigrated to Canada in 1997. She now lives in Vancouver, British Columbia.

For more information on all the books

in the Orca Currents line, please visit

orcabook.com